The AMAZING DAYS of ABBY HAYES

All That Glitters Isn't Gold

Read more books about me!

Read more sister stories!

Sister Magic

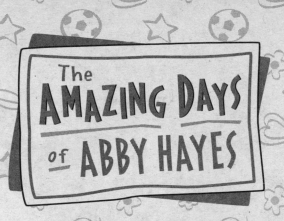

The AMAZING DAYS of ABBY HAYES

All That Glitters Isn't Gold

ANNE MAZER

SCHOLASTIC INC.
New York Toronto London Auckland Sydney
Mexico City New Delhi Hong Kong Buenos Aires

To Katie Machia

No part of this publication may be reproduced, stored in a retrieval system, or transmitted in any form or by any means, electronic, mechanical, photocopying, recording, or otherwise, without written permission of the publisher. For information regarding permission, write to Scholastic Inc., Attention: Permissions Department, 557 Broadway, New York, NY 10012.

ISBN-13: 978-0-439-82929-8
ISBN-10: 0-439-82929-1

Text copyright © 2009 by Anne Mazer
Illustrations copyright © 2009 by Scholastic Inc.
All rights reserved. Published by Scholastic Inc.

SCHOLASTIC, APPLE PAPERBACKS, THE AMAZING DAYS OF ABBY HAYES, and associated logos are trademarks and/or registered trademarks of Scholastic Inc.

12 11 10 9 8 7 6 5 4 3 2 1   9 10 11 12 13 14/0

Printed in the U.S.A.   40

First printing, May 2009

The AMAZING DAYS of ABBY HAYES

All That Glitters Isn't Gold

Chapter 1

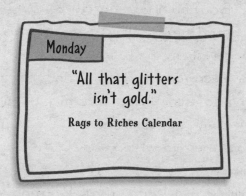

Monday

"All that glitters isn't gold."

Rags to Riches Calendar

List of Glittery Things That Aren't Gold:
My mother's sequined bag
Isabel's green glitter fingernail polish
Eva's baseball bat
Alex's metallic robots
My father's new laptop computer
My shiny new lunch box
Oh, yeah. And the cell phone that
Brianna is getting next week

P.S. If you don't know who Isabel, Eva,
Alex, and Brianna are, see the Who's Who
list below.

*　　*　　*

Lately, Brianna has talked of NOTHING but her brand-new cell phone. She is supposed to get it in a few days.

It has been one long Brianna brag fest.

Listening to her brag, you might think her cell phone will be solid gold. (I wouldn't put it past her to show up with a glittering golden phone!)

You might also think that Brianna's cell phone will be able to walk, talk, and recite the alphabet.

I bet Brianna thinks her phone can change skim milk to chocolate malted shakes, and turn cafeteria mystery mush to actual food!

Ha-ha. Just kidding.

Actually, Brianna's cell phone can "only" take pictures, make movies, search the Internet, give directions, send e-mail, and, oh, yeah, make phone calls.

According to her, it's got the latest and best in design technology.

It's called a Me-phone. (Of course.)

*　　*　　*

We interrupt this exciting update for a message from your sponsor.

Brianna, stop talking about your cell phone and all the things it can do!

WHO CARES?

There is more to life than cell phones!

Like writing in journals. And hanging out with friends. And arguing with your family!

Who's Who Around Here:

Isabel, irritating older sister of me, Abby Hayes. Isabel is a twin of Eva Hayes. She is an A+ student, a debate team head, a scholarship winner, a starring actress, and a fingernail polish nut.

Eva, un-identical twin to Isabel, and also an annoying older sister to me, Abby Hayes. A sports fanatic, the captain of the swim team, a basketball star, a lacrosse star, a softball star . . . you get the idea . . . she's good at sports.

Alex, younger brother of Abby, Isabel, and Eva. A somewhat less annoying sibling. He is obsessed with robots, math, and computers, a champion toy builder and an online gamer.

Brianna, my classmate. Star of the Universe. She rides horses, speaks French, and stars in commercials. She has the best, is the best, and gets the best. Also, she is the biggest bragger in sixth grade.

And hey, in case you haven't noticed — she's about to get a new cell phone.*

*Cell phone. Overrated tiny electronic device that fits in a pocket and allows parents to call their kids constantly.

"Abby! You won't believe what I got over the weekend!" Abby's best friend, Hannah, bounded across the hallway toward her.

Hannah's eyes were sparkling. Her smile was sparkling. Even her clothing was sparkling.

She was wearing a bright orange T-shirt and white cargo pants. Her sneakers were lime green.

"What?" Abby asked eagerly.

She couldn't help thinking that a few months ago, she would have heard Hannah's news by now.

She would have known before they reached the school.

Once, Abby and Hannah walked to school together every day. On the way, they shared all their news.

They told each other everything that happened since the last time they saw each other.

But when Abby's family moved to Misty Acres, the daily walks with Hannah, and other friends, had ended. Abby had to ride the school bus every day.

She missed seeing Hannah every morning. And, even worse, she had to put up with Brianna.

Brianna's family lived in the biggest and best house in Misty Acres. It sat on top of a hill where it looked down on the other, less impressive houses.

Every morning on the school bus, Abby got an extra daily dose of bragging. Brianna talked constantly about her fancy house, her expensive clothes, her horses, her plays, her commercials, her music. . . .

It didn't seem fair to Abby. When her family moved, she got more of Brianna and less of Hannah.

Abby wished it was the other way around.

Fortunately, Brianna was frequently chauffeured to school in her family's sleek new silver car.

Like today, for example.

Abby had enjoyed a peaceful bus ride. She had stared out the window and daydreamed. Before she knew it, the trip was over.

These days, she was always glad to get to school. It was where she got to see her friends without planning ahead of time.

Hannah tapped Abby on the shoulder. "Look," she said.

She unzipped an outside pocket on her backpack and took out a small rectangular object.

"Oh, no!" Abby groaned. "Not you, too!"

"Don't you like my new cell phone?" Hannah said, sounding surprised. "I thought you'd love it. It'll be so much easier for us to keep in touch."

"It's okay," Abby said, gritting her teeth. Then she burst out, "What's the big deal about cell phones? They're all anyone talks about!"

"Here's one reason why." Hannah flipped open her phone to show off a picture of her baby sister, Elena, on the screen.

Elena was adorable. Abby often wished she had a little sister like Elena, to follow her around and imitate everything she did.

"She's so cute! But why can't you just carry

a photo of her?" Abby said. "Why do you need a cell phone?"

"But look, Abby." Hannah pressed some buttons to show her a series of photos of her baby sister. "It's a camera *and* a cell phone. I can take pictures, too."

Abby shook her head. She wasn't impressed.

Well, maybe she was, a little . . .

"My parents don't worry about me as much now," Hannah went on. "They know they can reach me at any time. So I have more freedom."

"More freedom?" Abby scoffed. "You have less. Your parents can check up on you all the time."

Hannah smiled. "You've got it all mixed up. But you should get a cell phone, too."

"I don't want one," Abby said.

She had actually had a cell phone for a week when her family went to Paris. All the Hayes kids had them, in case they got lost.

That hadn't worked out very well. Abby had gotten lost and her cell phone had been stolen.

She had found her family again without any help from cell phones.

"Elena tried to throw my cell phone in the toilet last night." Hannah didn't seem able to talk about anything else. "Now I have to hide it from her. But it's so totally worth it."

"Is it?" Abby said. She was tired of the subject already.

But Hannah wasn't. "Do Isabel and Eva have cell phones?"

"No," Abby sighed.

"They don't?" Hannah repeated in surprise. "Why not?"

"My parents say they'd use them to fight with each other. I'm sure they're right. Can we change the subject?"

"Sure," Hannah said. She sounded a little hurt. But then Mason joined them.

"The cell phone is a weapon of mass destruction," he joked.

The formerly pudgy fifth grader had recently shot up. Now he was taller than Abby. He looked — and sometimes acted — like a totally different person. One who was not only nice, but almost good-looking.

"Do you have a cell phone, Mason?" Hannah asked him.

Abby hoped he didn't. She needed someone on her side.

Mason flipped his open. "Brand-new," he said.

"*Everyone* has a cell phone!" Abby cried.

It seemed as if it was all anyone talked about these days. But there was more to life than technology. There were friendships, family, sports, writing, books, travel, movies, music, and games. . . .

Abby had to admit that now that two of her best friends had cell phones, she felt a little left out.

"Let's text each other!" Hannah said to Mason.

Abby let out a long sigh. She slowly walked away.

Hannah and Mason didn't notice her leaving.

They were too busy texting, exchanging phone numbers, and showing off the features on their phones.

Chapter 2

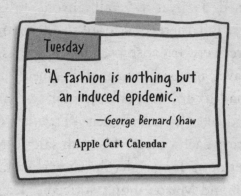

Tuesday

"A fashion is nothing but an induced epidemic."

—George Bernard Shaw

Apple Cart Calendar

Now that Brianna can't stop bragging about her next new technological wonder, and Hannah and Mason have cell phones, too, I've suddenly noticed how many people have them.

Cell phones are the newest fashion in my school. When I walk down the hall, I hear hundreds of different ringtones.

Practically every kid is holding a tiny rectangular device to their ear.

Practically every kid seems to be babbling to themselves.

Practically every kid ignores the other people nearby.

A Sampling of Cell "Conversations"

"Going to class."

"Whatchya doing? Oh, not much."

"I brought a tuna fish sandwich for lunch."

"What? Oh, yeah."

"Nothing."

Wow . . . Fascinating. (I'm being sarcastic. In case you didn't notice.)

They aren't conversations. They sound more like "Ramblings" or "Mutterings" or "Blah, Blah, Blahs." Or maybe "Blabberings."

Talking on a cell phone is a mass epidemic. It's a contagious illness.

Cellphonitis is sweeping through the school. . . .

Why hasn't it affected me, too?

I almost wish it would.

I hate feeling left out. It's no fun to be alone in a crowd.

It's no fun to hear everyone talking about things that I can't understand.

It's no fun to be practically the only person in the school who doesn't have a cell phone.

Even my friend Sophia has one. And so does Simon. And Natalie. And Lucas. And Bethany. And . . .

They ALL do!

Funny how I didn't notice it before. But now I do.

The day dragged on. Abby was glad when the last bell rang. The "Day of the Cell Phones" was finally over.

Did she want one?

Or did she not?

Abby wasn't sure.

She didn't know if she wanted to walk around all day with a few inches of plastic stuck to her ear.

She had always thought that cell phones were unnecessary, annoying, and silly. Her parents did, too.

Still, she couldn't help wanting to be part of the chattering crowd. . . .

Or wanting to program her friends' numbers into her phone.

Or wanting to take pictures of everyone's shoelaces or pets or new haircut with her cell camera.

Or wanting to video a soccer game on her cell.

But even if she decided that she wanted one, she'd still have a serious problem.

She'd have to convince her parents to get one for her.

Abby opened her locker door and began to stack her books inside.

"Abby!" Hannah was hurrying toward her.

Abby's mood brightened. Even if Hannah had a cell phone now, she was still her best friend.

Nothing could change that.

"How was your day?" Hannah asked her.

"So-so," Abby replied.

"I know you don't want to hear this," Hannah began. "But you *have* to convince your parents to get you a cell phone!"

Abby let out a long breath.

"I can guess how you feel," Hannah said sympathetically. "A week ago, I was just like you. I thought cell phones were just a fad. But now that I have one, I love it."

"I can see that," Abby said drily.

"Do you mind talking about this?" Hannah asked. Abby shook her head.

"If you had a cell phone, it would be so much easier to stay in touch," Hannah continued. "We could text each other all the time. And we could talk whenever we felt like it. Just like we used to. Wouldn't that be great?"

Abby couldn't help agreeing. "Eva and Isabel are always hogging the phone," she said.

"I know!" Hannah cried. "You can only make phone calls when they're at practices or rehearsals."

Last year, when Abby and Hannah wanted to talk and the lines were busy, they had hurried over to each other's houses.

They couldn't do that anymore now that Abby lived in Misty Acres. To see each other now, they had to figure out schedules; they had to make dates; they had to arrange rides.

Or Abby had to wait for the phone to be free.

"Ask your parents," Hannah urged. "Tell them you need a cell, too."

A cell sounded better and better. Abby would have instant access to her friends. She could call Hannah from anywhere. She'd be able to stay on the phone as long as she liked. And, of course, her parents could reach her in emergencies.

"Maybe I'll talk to them," Abby said slowly.

"Yes!" Hannah pumped her fist in the air. "I knew you would!"

"But they won't agree," Abby warned. "They don't believe in buying us things they don't think we need."

"You can convince them. I have faith in you," Hannah said. "Just try."

Hannah's cell phone buzzed loudly. She glanced at the display. "Sorry. Have to take this one."

"I'll talk to you later," Abby said. "If I can. . . ."

Hannah waved and hurried down the hall, talking on her cell phone.

Suddenly, Abby knew what she wanted. She wanted a cell phone. She wanted one as soon as possible.

I don't care if it's the most plain, ordinary cell phone, she said fiercely to herself. *I'll take one without a camera or online games. I just want to stay more in touch with my friends.*

Her parents knew how isolated she often felt at Misty Acres. They would understand.

And Abby would offer to help pay for the phone. She'd do dish duty. She'd clean sinks. She'd even scrub floors if she had to.

She slammed her locker door shut and started walking toward the exit. A cluster of students was blocking the door.

Brianna emerged from the crowd like a queen.

She was wearing a gold miniskirt and a white flounced blouse. She had sheepskin boots on her feet.

"Abby!" she said. "I've been waiting for you."

"You have?" Abby said in confusion.

Half the time, Brianna didn't even acknowledge Abby existed. She only talked to her on the school bus when she needed an audience.

"I got my Me-phone a week early. I thought you'd be dying to see it. Everyone is."

"Is today National Show Off Your Cell Phone Day?" Abby said under her breath.

Abby had to admit, she *was* curious. Was Brianna's Me-phone that much better than Hannah's or Mason's?

Brianna opened her leather backpack. "It's just the kind of thoughtful thing I'm known for," she said. "Besides, now that you live in Misty Acres, you should always aim for The Best. Not that you'd ever get a Me-phone. But you can dream."

Abby rolled her eyes.

Brianna whipped out the Me-phone.

"Look at this beauty!" she exclaimed. "And I'm not talking about me," she added. "Though, of course, I might be."

"I'm really not interested in your Me-phone," Abby began to say. "It's just another talking device." And then she saw it.

It fit in the palm of Brianna's manicured hand.

The Me-phone was a slim rectangle of gleaming, hi-tech loveliness. It was small, sleek, and shining.

Without a moment's hesitation, Abby fell head over heels in love with it.

Chapter 3

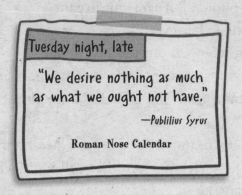

What I ought not have:

A Me-phone, of course

I want Brianna's Me-phone.

I desire it more than anything!

It hurts to write these words. In fact, I
can hardly believe that I'm writing them!
I wish it wasn't so.

It's one thing to want an ordinary cell
phone to keep in touch with your friends.
It's another to want a Me-phone.

Do I, Abby Hayes, actually want

something called a Me-phone? Even the name is stupid and annoying.

Couldn't I want a You-phone or a Blue-phone, a She-phone, a Spot-phone, a Not-phone, or even a plain old cell phone?

No, of course not.

It's the Me-phone or nothing.

I MUST have it. Even if it costs six hundred dollars.

The above words were written by Abby Hayes at ten thirty last night when she should have been in bed.

Abby Hayes solemnly avows that no one forced her to write these words.

She was of sound body and mind when she took pen to paper.

No one bribed her, fed her bowls of cheese popcorn and cotton candy, or otherwise improperly influenced her.

Abby, and Abby alone, is responsible for this journal entry.

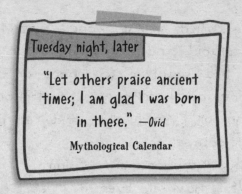

"Let others praise ancient
times; I am glad I was born
in these." —Ovid

Mythological Calendar

When my parents were kids, in ancient
times, they had only television, movies, radio,
and tape recorders.

There were no computers, electronic games,
DVD players, CDs, digital cameras, portable
media players, cell phones. . . .

What did they do all day?

Play marbles? Memorize math problems?

Thank goodness I was born in
these times.

I've grown up with technology.
I know how to e-mail, search
online, play computer games,
and take digital photos.

Brianna's Me-phone does all that
and more!

Hooray for Today! Hooray for Technology! Hooray! Hooray!

This is a message from the one percent of Abby's brain that isn't swooning over the Me-phone.
ARE YOU DONE NOW?
ENOUGH ALREADY!
Go back to your old cell-phone-hating self!
No? I didn't think so.
Then go back to the Abby who would have been completely satisfied with a simple, modest, ordinary phone.

But I can't. . . .
I REALLY want a Me-phone.
I want it so bad, it hurts.

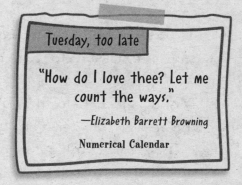

Tuesday, too late

"How do I love thee? Let me count the ways."
—Elizabeth Barrett Browning
Numerical Calendar

1. I love your little ringtones.
2. I love your cool, shiny design.
3. I love your wide screen.
4. I love your buttons.
5. I love your functions.
6. I love your pale, glittery colors.
7. I love your perfection and your total cool.
8. You are the It-phone!
9. I love everything about you, Me-phone! I wish you were My-phone!!!

TUESDAY, NEVER MIND HOW LATE:

I'm dreaming of my Me-phone and me.

Dream #1: I pull it out in the hallway and everyone interrupts their conversations to gawk.

Dream #2: I flash it in my classrooms. The teachers stop the lesson to ask to take a look at it.

Dream #3: I show it off to the ultra-cool seventh and eighth graders on the staff of The Daisy. They all want to hang out with me.

Dream #4: I stand on the street corner. Everyone wonders about the mysterious girl with the curly red hair who's talking on her Me-phone.

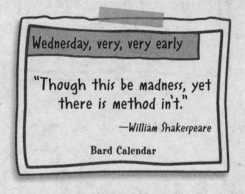

Wednesday, very, very early

"Though this be madness, yet there is method in't."

—William Shakespeare

Bard Calendar

Have: Madness.
Need: Method.

I haven't asked my parents to get me any cell phone yet. That's going to be hard enough.

It's going to be next to impossible to convince them to get me a Me-phone.

Must figure out a way!

Need method for my madness.

Will stay awake until I find it.

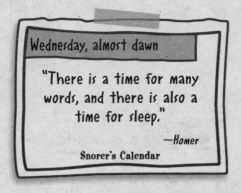

Wednesday, almost dawn

"There is a time for many words, and there is also a time for sleep."

—Homer

Snorer's Calendar

Tonight I've written many, many words.

And I've missed the time for sleep.

It's time to get up already.

Maybe I'll lie down and close my eyes for a few minutes before breakfast.

If I had a Me-phone, I could set the alarm to wake me up.

If I had a Me-phone, I wouldn't need

to stay up all night planning and hoping
and dreaming.

If I had a Me-phone, I might be able
to think about something else for a change.

Will this convince my parents to get me one?

Chapter 4

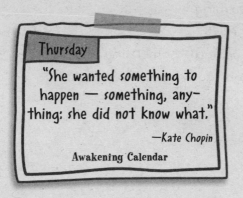

Yes, I want something to happen. And I DO know what it is.

If you've read the last journal entry, so do you!

"You want what?" Abby's father said. He was so sur-prised that he dropped a baked potato onto his lap.

"Good one, Dad!" Alex cheered.

His father speared the potato with his fork and plopped it back on his plate. "Lucky I didn't butter it yet," he said.

"Dad, you need a bib," Isabel commented.

"Or a plastic shield," Alex said.

"Or maybe fewer shocking requests from a certain middle-school daughter," their father said.

"Dad!" Abby protested. "What's so shocking about wanting a cell phone?"

If they thought *this* was shocking, what would they think about a Me-phone?

Abby had decided to take things slowly. First, she'd get them used to the basic idea.

She could already tell that this wasn't going to be easy.

Then, when her parents had accepted the idea of cell phones in the Hayes family, she'd carefully lead the conversation toward the Me-phone.

It was a really good plan, Abby thought. If only she could present it to a different family!

"It's not the cell phone that's shocking," her mother said now. "It's the person who asked for it."

"This isn't you, Abby," her father said, shaking his head. "I would never have expected *you* to ask for a cell phone."

"Yeah, you're the one who doesn't like computers and electronics," Alex said. "You have gadget-phobia."

"So? People change," Abby said, a bit defensively.

Her family had no idea how much she had *really* changed.

"But this isn't normal," Eva said. "Let me guess. You're trying to impress a boy. . . ."

"I'm not!" Abby cried, her face turning red.

She had once had a crush on Simon, who played saxophone in the Jazz Tones. But they were friends now.

"Or maybe you want to have private conversations that no one can overhear," Isabel suggested.

"Don't *you*?" Abby retorted.

Her older sister smirked in a superior way.

Abby ignored her. "I just want a cell phone," she said again.

Couldn't her family understand this simple concept? If not, her secret hopes were doomed.

"I want to talk to Hannah," Abby continued. "I want to keep in touch with my friends. It's all about communication. And not feeling all alone."

They were her best arguments, but her parents didn't respond.

"I'm willing to work for it," Abby added.

"No one else in the Hayes family has a cell phone," her father pointed out. "Except your mother. And she needs it for work."

"Besides, Abby can't have one if Eva and I don't," Isabel said.

Eva nodded in a rare moment of unity with her twin. "That's right."

"As the older sisters, we should be first," Isabel said.

"Then we should *all* get cell phones!" Abby said.

"Yes!" Alex agreed. "Now you're talking!"

"Now *we're* talking," Abby said. "We have to stick together."

If the Hayes siblings united, she had a chance. But Eva and Isabel were out only for themselves.

"Oldest first," they chanted.

Paul Hayes held up his hand. "Now wait a minute, everyone. Don't get carried away."

"I don't understand this sudden need for cell phones," their mother said. "We've done fine without them until now."

"More and more kids have them today," Abby argued. "Even Hannah and Mason do. It's all they talk about."

"Or on," Isabel snickered.

"That's not a good enough reason," her father said. "You kids don't need to have everything your friends do."

Eva shrugged. "I can live without a cell phone."

"Me, too," Isabel said.

"But I can't!" Abby cried, glaring at her sisters. "Didn't you go to middle school, Dad? Mom? Didn't you want things, too? Haven't you ever felt left out?"

Her parents exchanged a glance. So did Eva and Isabel.

"A cell phone *would* save our family lots of time." Isabel swiftly and unexpectedly switched over to Abby's side.

"Especially until we start driving," Eva added.

"What if we need one during an emergency?" Isabel argued. "What if the bus breaks down? What if my ride home from play rehearsal doesn't show up?"

"What if I sprain my ankle in lacrosse practice?" Eva asked.

Abby gave her older sisters a thumbs-up.

"What if I got lost biking?" Alex added. "What if school closed in the middle of the day?"

"What if I got sick in school?" Eva asked.

"A cell phone would keep us all safer," Isabel concluded. "It would give us peace of mind."

Abby looked at her siblings with pride. They had taken awhile to come over to her side, but once they did, they were a force to be reckoned with.

Maybe they'd want Me-phones, too?

Better not to bring *that* up just yet.

"Kids grew up for millions of years without cell phones," their father argued. "You'll live for a few more years without them."

"If there's an emergency, you can call on someone else's phone," their mother said firmly.

"But that's so pathetic!" Eva said. "It screams *loser*."

Their mother shook her head. "As far as I'm concerned, a cell phone is just another overpriced piece of equipment to lose."

"Multiply that by four kids and a monthly plan for all of us," her father said, "and we're talking thousands of dollars."

What were they going to say about the six-hundred-dollar Me-phone? But then, Abby would pay for it herself — even if she had to give up her allowance until she was in college.

"We're not poor!" Isabel said. "We just moved to a bigger house!"

"That's right," Abby echoed. "You didn't complain about money when we went to Paris."

"Paris was different," their mother said.

"How?" Eva demanded.

Their father spooned sour cream onto his plate. "May I point out that, only thirty minutes ago, none of you wanted cell phones. Except Abby."

"We do now," the Hayes children chorused.

Do I ever, Abby added silently.

Their parents exchanged another long glance.

"Okay, we'll think about it," their father said finally.

"But don't get your hopes up," their mother said.

"Any old cell phone will do," Isabel begged. "Even one without a camera."

"That's right," Eva said. "We don't need anything fancy."

"Yeah," Alex said.

Only Abby was silent. She was suddenly worried that she might have gone about this the wrong way.

"No!" Abby cried. "Any old phone won't do for me."

"What do you mean?" her mother asked. "What kind of a cell phone *do* you want?"

Abby looked down at her plate. Her face was burning. But what did she have to lose? It was all or nothing now.

She lifted her head. "I want a Me-phone," she said in a defiant voice. "A nice purple Me-phone."

Chapter 5

My family didn't waste their day today.
And they can thank me for it.

When I said that I wanted a Me-
phone, everyone laughed hysterically.

They didn't stop for a good ten minutes.

Hayes Family Howler

Eva and Isabel were screaming with
laughter.

My father practically choked on his baked
potato.

Alex spit out his milk.

My mother laughed so hard that she had tears coming out of her eyes.

The only person who was unmoved was me, Abby Hayes. I didn't laugh at all. My day was wasted.

Yes, I told them that I wanted a six-hundred-dollar, sleek, glittering, up-to-the-moment technological shrine of genius.

Yes, I'm only a sixth grader.

And, yes, I know that I don't <u>need</u> a six-hundred-dollar phone.

And, yes, I knew that my family would never understand. (Even <u>I</u> have a hard time understanding it!)

But did they have to act like they had just heard the funniest joke of their lives?

Did they have to howl quite so loudly?

They didn't even say they were sorry.

Instead, every time they looked at me, they burst out laughing again.

* * *

That wasn't the worst of it, though.

When they stopped laughing, they started using logic on me.

Hayes Family Logic:

1. "It costs a fortune, stupid!" Isabel Hayes

2. "Even if you had the money, why waste it on a Me-phone?" Isabel again

3. "You're just a sixth grader. Me-phones are meant for wealthy adults. Or obsessed geeks." Eva Hayes

4. "You'd never figure out how to use it." Alex Hayes

5. "You don't _really_ need a cell phone at all." Paul Hayes

6. "Me-phones only work with one plan. And it's a plan we'd never get." Olivia Hayes

7. "A Me-phone is something that Brianna would have." Isabel Hayes, getting dangerously close to the truth

8. "Abby imitate Brianna? Ha ha ha ha ha ha!" Eva Hayes

9. "If Abby got a Me-phone, we'd all get them, right?" Alex Hayes, wistfully

10. "No one is getting a Me-phone around here. And that's final." Olivia Hayes

My family can laugh.
They can ridicule.
They can use logic.
They can say, "The decision is final."
But they won't change my mind.

The Me-phone is everything that is cool and stylish and modern. I want the Me-phone to be mine. I want the Me-phone to be ME.

When I write in my journal, I think about it. When I close my eyes, I see it. Whether I'm awake or asleep, I dream of it.

Maybe it doesn't make sense for me to want it, but I do. I want a Me-phone more than anything.

As Abby climbed into the school bus on Friday morning, she looked around for Brianna.

But Brianna wasn't there. Abby felt let down.

Was this really her? she wondered. Had it come to this? Was she looking forward to Brianna's bragging?

"It's all because of the Me-phone," she murmured. "This is what it's done to me."

At the thought of the Me-phone, Abby felt a wave of longing.

She wanted, no, she *had* to see the Me-phone.

She had to hold it in her hands.

She had to gaze at its screen and scroll through its options.

Was five minutes too much to ask?

Unfortunately, it all depended on Brianna. If she wasn't on the bus, neither was the Me-phone.

Abby plunked herself down in a seat and stared moodily out the window.

Suddenly, she heard the sweet sound of boasting.

". . . My starring role . . . movie producer . . . my brilliant role . . . the best they'd ever seen . . . blah, blah, blah . . ."

Abby's eyes lit up. She swiveled around.

"Brianna!" She waved wildly. "Over here!"

Brianna tottered over on high heels. She slid into the seat next to Abby and began to brag.

"I have a very special treat for you," she began. "You can watch *my* commercial on the Me-phone. Over three hundred girls auditioned for the part that *I* won. . . ."

Brianna touched a few buttons and then handed the Me-phone to Abby.

"Thank you," Abby breathed. She couldn't believe that Brianna was letting her hold the Me-phone. She'd watch a thousand commercials for that.

"When we're done with this one, there's more of me," Brianna said.

Abby concentrated on the tiny images streaming on the Me-phone screen.

If she had a Me-phone, she could view clips of her favorite television shows.

She could take photos and e-mail them to all her friends.

She could listen to music, she could play online games, she could get maps of her neighborhood if she got lost, she could record her voice, and she could . . .

". . . see my professional head shots," Brianna was saying. "They're stored on my phone, in case I need to e-mail them to television producers."

"Amazing," Abby whispered. "And so perfect."

Brianna looked pleased. "I am," she agreed.

Abby didn't correct her.

"I can Google myself, too," Brianna went on. "I do it every night. I can also show you my fan sites."

"Sure, I'd love to see them," Abby said.

She pinched herself, just to make sure it was really her who was saying that. Would Abby really look at *anything* on the Me-phone, even Brianna's fan sites, just to hold the Me-phone and to pretend, for a few brief moments, that it was hers?

She'd never put up with Brianna's boasting before. She'd always made fun of it. And here she was encouraging it.

It was all because of the Me-phone! It was a few square inches of wonder. Abby had to experience every inch of it.

Especially if she had to wait until she was an adult to have one.

"*You'd* like a Me-phone, too, wouldn't you?" Brianna said, almost as if she knew what Abby was thinking. As if she knew what Abby's parents had already said.

"Yes," Abby admitted. "But please don't tell anyone."

She didn't want her friends to laugh at her the way her family had. She didn't want them to tell her she was crazy.

But Brianna didn't laugh at her.

This is *crazy*, Abby thought. It was as if Brianna, of all people, understood.

Chapter 6

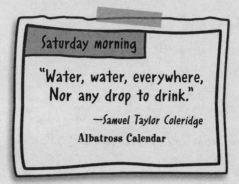

Saturday morning

"Water, water, everywhere,
Nor any drop to drink."

—Samuel Taylor Coleridge
Albatross Calendar

I see cell phones everywhere. **Everywhere!**

All my friends have cell phones.

All our neighbors have them.

My teachers have them.

The principal has one.

The school bus driver has one.

People on the streets have them.

They hang from belts, they're kept in purses, they're hidden in pockets, and they're attached to ears.

Their ringtones are everywhere.

I can't walk down the street without

hearing, seeing, and sometimes touching cell phones.

It makes me want a cell phone more than ever. Why does everyone have a cell phone but ME!!!

Would I have been better off with <u>any</u> cell phone rather than none? Today I think so.

Today I think I shouldn't have asked for a Me-phone.

Today I think that I should have agreed with my siblings and pretended that I, too, wanted a "plain, ordinary phone."

Today I think that maybe then my parents would have come over to our side.

Don't get me wrong.

I still love the Me-phone. I want the Me-phone. I'm crazy about the Me-phone.

But today I wish I had a cell phone, any old kind!

It was Saturday morning. The Hayes siblings were getting ready to leave for weekend clubs, meetings, practices, and other activities.

"We have to go soon," Isabel said. She blew on her freshly polished glittering green fingernails.

"The drama meeting starts at ten sharp," she added. "I'm in charge and I can't be late."

Eva bent over to lace up her running shoes. Her ponytail flopped in her face. "I'm supposed to be on the field doing warm-ups in twenty minutes," she said.

Alex zipped his backpack and glanced at the clock. "I have to be on the bus in half an hour for the computer club trip."

"Dad!" Three impatient voices cried at the same time. "Hurry up!"

"Relax, everyone," their father said. He strolled into the kitchen, picked up his wallet and keys, and smiled at his offspring. "There's still plenty of time."

"Says who?" Eva demanded.

"This is no time for jokes," Isabel said.

"I *can't* be late," Alex said.

Only Abby was silent. Alone out of the four Hayes siblings, she was still in her pajamas.

She sat at the breakfast table and spooned sugar onto her cereal. There was an open paperback book in front of her.

Her father counted the money in his wallet. Then he glanced at Abby. "What are your plans for today?" he asked.

"This morning I'm staying home," Abby said. "This afternoon, Hannah, Sophia, and I are going to a matinee. Can you give me a ride to the movie theater at four forty-five?"

Her father nodded. "No problem, honey."

"Remember, you have to pick *me* up at three thirty from my play practice," Isabel said.

"My game should be done at four," Eva said. "Unless we go into overtime."

"The bus gets in from the museum at five fifteen," Alex said.

Their father sighed. "It would be a lot easier if your mother didn't have to work today," he said.

"Is she at work already?" Isabel said.

"Yes," their father said, rubbing his forehead. "I wish she was around to help out today. But don't worry, I can keep it all straight."

"You know, if we'd stayed in our old house . . ." Abby began.

"Not this again, Abby!" Isabel cried.

Abby put down her spoon. She was more attached

to their old house and their former neighborhood than anyone else in the family.

The house at Misty Acres was closer to her mother's new law office. It had a spacious new kitchen, a family room, and a private home office for her father.

Abby's room had a writing loft, and she didn't have to share a bathroom with her sisters anymore.

But she'd trade all of it for her old house, any day.

Eva glanced at the clock. "We have to leave *now*," she said. She picked up her sports bag. "I'm going out to the car."

"Me, too," Isabel said.

"Me, too, too," Alex said.

They followed Eva out of the house.

"I'll pick you up at four forty-five sharp," her father said to Abby. "Be ready at the front door."

"You bet, Dad!"

The door slammed behind him. A moment later, Abby heard the sound of the car pulling out of the driveway.

She stretched luxuriously. She was the only one in the family who didn't have to rush out of the house on this Saturday morning.

She was planning a relaxed day at home.

First, she was going to read and write in her journal.

In the afternoon, she'd walk around outside for a little while, and then get ready to meet Hannah and Sophia at the movie theater.

Afterward, they'd all hang out together. Hannah had invited her two friends to have dinner at her house.

Abby was really looking forward to spending time with her friends in the old neighborhood.

Maybe they'd stroll around after dinner, say hello to Mason or other kids who lived nearby.

And maybe Abby would check out everyone's cell phones and see how they compared with Brianna's.

She'd write their numbers down, for when she got *her* cell phone.

Abby sighed. It didn't seem likely that she'd get one, not even if she bought it herself.

And a Me-phone was completely out of reach.

"When I'm grown up," Abby promised herself, "the first thing I'll do is buy a Me-phone."

Although, by then, there would probably be something even better.

Chapter 7

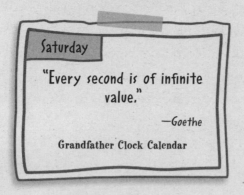

I enjoyed every second of this day.
I read and wrote in my loft.
Then I took a shower and got dressed.
I listened to music.
Dad came home after dropping every-
one off. He checked in on me and
then went out to do the weekly food
shopping.

When he came home again, I helped him
put away the groceries. Then we had lunch
together.

After lunch, Dad left for the third time
today. He had a long list of errands to do,

but he promised to be back here at four forty-five sharp, after picking up Isabel and Eva, and before getting Alex.

Then I took a walk, watched a TV show, and wrote a letter.

I enjoyed every second of this day — until now.

It is now four forty-five.

I am standing at the front door, just like I promised.

But Dad isn't here. His car isn't pulling into the driveway.

He has to be here SOON or I will miss the movie!

4:48 p.m. Dad is three minutes late. Tapping my foot impatiently.

4:51 p.m. Come on, already!

4:52 p.m. Has he gotten stuck in traffic?

4:53 p.m. If he gets here soon, I can still make the movie.

4:56 p.m. If we had cell phones, he could call me.

4:59 p.m. If I had a cell phone, I could call HIM.

5:00 p.m. If I had a cell phone, I could call Hannah and Sophia.

5:01 p.m. Are Hannah and Sophia wondering where I am? Are they getting annoyed with me?

5:06 p.m. Dad, where are you??

5:12 p.m. The inside phone is ringing! I hope it's Dad! I hope he's on his way!

5:14 p.m. It was Hannah and Sophia. They used Hannah's cell phone to call me. They can't wait for me any longer. They're going into the movie. . . .

5:15 p.m. Dad is half an hour late. I've definitely missed the movie.

5:22 p.m. Now I'm starting to worry.

5:27 p.m. I call Mom at her office. Dad is fine, as far as she knows.

5:28 p.m. I'm mad.

5:32 p.m. I'm REALLY mad.

5:33 p.m. Stomp upstairs to my room. Climb up to my writing loft with journal.

5:37 p.m. Wipe tearstains off journal.

5:39 p.m. Blow nose loudly.

5:46 p.m. Sixty-one minutes late! Hear car in garage. Rush downstairs.

5:48 p.m. Three unhappy Hayes siblings storm into the kitchen. Everyone is yelling. It seems as if Dad was either too late or too early for all of them.

5:50 p.m. I tell them they're lucky they got rides. I say that Dad never showed up for me at all. They don't even hear me.

5:53 p.m. Dad enters kitchen.

5:53 p.m. Dad sees me, throws up his hands, cries, "Oh, no! I'm SO sorry, Abby! I forgot all about you!"

5:54 p.m. I yell, "You made me miss the movie!" Then I burst into tears again.

5:55 p.m. Siblings comfort me.

6:01 p.m. Isabel says to Dad, "If we had cell phones, none of this would have happened."

6:02 p.m. Eva agrees.

6:03 p.m. Alex agrees.

6:04 p.m. I agree.

6:06 p.m. Dad agrees. But he doesn't agree to get us cell phones.

6:35 p.m. Dad drives me to Hannah's

house for dinner. He apologizes all the
way there.

I argue for cell phones all the way there.
(Not a Me-phone. I'm going after what
I might actually get.)

But, of course, Dad still says no.

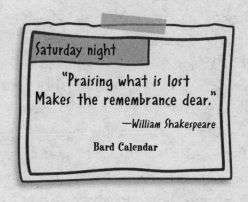

Saturday night

"Praising what is lost
Makes the remembrance dear."

—William Shakespeare

Bard Calendar

I was looking forward to a great evening
with Hannah and Sophia.

I WASN'T looking forward to hours and
hours of conversation about a movie that I
didn't see.

But Hannah and Sophia couldn't stop
raving about it.

It was the best movie they'd ever seen.

The movie was so funny, clever, exciting, and romantic.

The actors were great. The scenes were hilarious. The story was gripping.

And blah, blah, blah . . .

Maybe all that praise "made the remembrance of the movie dear" for Hannah and Sophia, but it only reminded ME of what I had lost.

Yes, I can see the movie another time, but I lost my chance to see it with Hannah and Sophia.

I lost the chance to eat a huge bucket of popcorn with them, to giggle over the funny lines together, and to talk about it afterward.

But most of all, their conversation reminded me that if I still lived in the old neighborhood, I wouldn't have lost anything.

I would have walked to Hannah's house instead of waiting for my father. And I would have gone to the movie with my two friends.

*   *   *

"Can we stop talking about the movie, already?" I said. "Remember, I wasn't there."

Hannah and Sophia both said they were sorry.

The movie would have been even better, they said, if I had been there.

They promised to talk about something else.

And we did — about cell phones.

I told them how my siblings and I were trying to convince our parents to get us cell phones.

Hannah and Sophia cheered me on.

They showed me their cell phones and gave me a short lesson in how they worked.

They weren't as nice as Brianna's Me-phone. But what is?

Sophia asked me what kind of cell I wanted.

"Whatever my parents will buy me," I said. And then I added, "There's a phone I REALLY want. But I'll never get it."

"Think positive," Hannah said. "You've got to believe!"

I shook my head. "My parents will never buy me a Me-phone."

Both my friends stared at me.

"You want a Me-phone?" Hannah said. "It's six hundred dollars. Abby Hayes, are you out of your mind?"

Sophia started giggling.

Then Hannah joined in.

It was my family all over again.

Except that now it was my best friends, too. Was Brianna the only person who could understand my love of the Me-phone?

And what did that say about me?

"What's so funny about wanting a Me-phone?" I asked. "Seriously . . . it's the best phone there is."

"Sorry," Hannah said. "It's just so unlike you, Abby."

"Like you're someone we don't even know," Sophia added.

I couldn't help saying, "Maybe you don't know me that well."

There was an awkward silence.

Then Sophia said, "Besides, you don't need a Me-phone. A normal phone will do whatever you need it to do."

"I'll be happy if my parents get me <u>any</u> cell phone," I cried. "But why can't I dream about a Me-phone, anyway? What's wrong with that?"

"Nothing, I guess," Hannah said. "But don't tell anyone."

I shrugged. "I only told Brianna."

"BRIANNA?" they both screeched. "What were you thinking?"

I couldn't explain myself anymore.

For almost the first time in my life, I didn't want to be with Hannah and Sophia. I wanted to go home.

If I still lived in my old neighborhood, I would have walked out then. But I had to wait for my father to pick me up.

I got up and faced my friends.

"Cell phones are supposed to bring us together," I said defiantly. "Why do they keep driving me apart from people?"

Chapter 8

Sunday

"The most astonishing thing about miracles is that they happen."

—G. K. Chesterton

Serendipitous Sayings Daybook

Yes, miracles happen.
They are real.
And it is astonishing!!

<u>Hayes Family Miracle</u>:
We are getting cell phones today!

Repeat after me: We are getting cell phones today!

We are getting cell phones today!

We are getting cell phones today!

I can't believe it!
I am dazed, amazed, and crazed with
hope!!!

How did this happen?
What changed my parents' mind?
Why, after saying no for so long, did
they finally say yes?
Do I have to know?
Do I even care?

The important fact is that, after today, I
will have my very own cell phone!
I will be like everyone else!
I will be able to call, text, and take photos!
I will get calls in the middle of lunch
and will have to shut off my ringer before
class.
I will walk down the street with my
ear glued to my phone. I will always be
checking it for messages.

I know it won't be a Me-phone, but
I hope to get a good one, anyway. If I

have to, I'll pay for extra features out of
my allowance.
HOORAY!!!!

The Hayes family van turned off the highway and
onto the mall road.

"There it is!" Alex said. He bounced up and down
on the seat. "The cell phone store!"

"Take the next right," Eva said.

"Oh! I can't wait!" Abby cried.

Isabel studied her nail polish. She was as excited as
everyone else, but she didn't like to show it.

"Calm down, everyone," their mother said.
"Remember, we're getting basic phones and a
basic plan."

"I have money saved. I can pay for extras," Abby
offered.

Their father pulled into the parking lot. He turned
off the ignition. Then he faced his four children.

"Let's get something straight before we go into
the store," he said. "It's one plan, one phone for
everyone."

Eva shrugged. "At least we're getting cell phones."

"Finally," Isabel agreed.

"I get a cell phone, too, right?" Alex demanded.

His mother turned to ruffle his hair. "That's right, sweetie."

Only Abby was silent. She was thinking hard.

Once she had a cell phone, her father would never forget to pick her up again. That was wonderful.

But she wanted so much more. . . . Why wouldn't they let her pay for what she wanted?

"Does everyone understand?" their father asked. "Are we all on the same page?"

"Yes," three of the four Hayes siblings said.

"Abby?" her mother asked.

"I know you won't get me a Me-phone," Abby said slowly. "But I want more than a basic phone and I don't understand why I can't get it. Especially since I'm willing to put down my own money. It's just not fair!"

"*Don't ruin this for everyone else!*" Isabel hissed.

"I can't believe you, Abby," Eva said furiously. "*You* were the one who wanted phones for all of us. Now you're going to wreck it."

"I thought you would be the happiest member of the Hayes family today," her mother said.

"You aren't *really* serious about a Me-phone, are you?" her father said. "I mean, it's a joke, right?"

Abby took a deep breath. "I really, really want a Me-phone," she said. "But I'll settle for a great cell phone, with all the features."

"*Settle* for a great cell phone?" Isabel said sarcastically. "How nice of you."

"We're definitely not getting one of those fancy, hyped, overpriced cell phones," her mother said. "And we're not even *close* to talking about a Me-phone."

"This isn't like you, Abby," her father said with a frown. "What's going on?"

"She's become a Brianna clone," Eva accused.

"I have *not*!" Abby cried.

She hoped with all her heart that it wasn't true.

But what if the desire for a Me-phone, or even a fancy cell phone, was the first step toward Brianna clone-dom?

Maybe Abby would start wearing miniskirts and makeup next. She'd audition for commercials, brag about her awards, flirt with every boy she met, and always have to be the best.

Abby let out a long breath. She really didn't think that was going to happen.

"Why can't you accept that I want a great cell phone?" Abby said to her family. "Even if you don't agree with it, you don't have to jump all over me. Don't I have the right to fight for what I want?"

Her sisters looked at each other and shrugged.

"Fair enough," Isabel said.

"Yeah, you're right," Eva admitted. "Sorry about that, Abby."

Abby stared at her twin sisters in astonishment. Was it true? Had they just apologized to her?

Had they actually admitted that they were in the wrong?

She wanted to savor the moment, but her parents had opened their doors and were getting out of the car.

"Enough talking," her father said. "It's time to buy some cell phones."

Chapter 9

Sunday

"Great minds have purposes,
others have wishes."

—Washington Irving

Hot Air Balloon Calendar

My parents have purposes.

<u>Parental Purpose</u>:

To get us the most basic cell phone plan,
with the most basic cell phone.

NOTE: If I had a dollar for every time
they've said "basic" today, I would have
enough money to buy a Me-phone.

I have wishes. (You know what they are.)

If my parents truly had great minds, they
would grant my wishes.

They won't, of course.

But I wish they would, because I'm sick of wanting. I'm sick of hoping. I'm sick of wishing!

I wish I had my wish, so I could stop wishing that my wishes would come true.

Oh, never mind!

Everyone else is already in the cell phone store. I better hurry up and join them.

"We want your simplest plan, with the fewest minutes," Olivia Hayes said to the cell phone customer service specialist.

"Is this for the entire family?" he asked the Hayes parents.

"All six of us," Paul Hayes said.

The four siblings crowded around the counter.

"That customer-whatever guy is cute," Eva whispered. She patted her hair.

Isabel gave her a *don't embarrass me in public* look.

"Let me show you your options," the customer service specialist began.

"We don't want options," Olivia Hayes interrupted. "We want something very simple and basic."

"Basic," Abby repeated. There was that word again.

"There's nothing wrong with basic," her mother said.

"Our most economical family plan offers twelve hundred free minutes," the customer service specialist said.

He unfolded a brightly colored brochure. "This chart compares our family plans. Your teenagers will want text messaging. . . ."

Paul Hayes shook his head. "Not for us."

"But, Dad . . ." Isabel said.

"We have to text!" Eva said.

"Yeah," Abby and Alex agreed.

"I understand how you feel," their father said. "But your mother and I are going to make the decisions here."

"No extra text messaging," Olivia Hayes said to the customer service specialist.

Abby glanced at her brother and older sisters. They seemed disappointed, but they only shrugged.

After all, their parents had made their intentions clear.

"Why don't you four kids go look at the phones?" Paul Hayes suggested. "We'll figure out the rest."

"What's the point of looking if we can't choose?" Abby grumbled.

But she really did want to check out the cell phones. Would any of them compare to the Me-phone?

Was there even the smallest chance that she could still convince her parents to buy something she wanted?

She and her siblings trailed over to the cell phone display.

Isabel made a beeline for a bright turquoise phone. "You can make videos on this one," she said.

"Look, you can watch sports TV on this one," Eva said. "But it's so tiny!"

"I've got a space communicator!" Alex cried, holding up a sleek silver model.

It seemed as if there were cell phones for every purpose — except maybe cooking dinner, or driving to the mall.

Abby lingered over a phone that came with a wireless headset, a leather case, and Internet connections. It also had a camera, a video camera, games, and lots of ringtones.

It wasn't the Me-phone, but it wasn't bad.

Abby looked at the price tag. It was over three hundred and fifty dollars. There was no way her parents would buy it.

What if Abby begged, borrowed from her savings,

or promised to pay them back for the next thirty years . . . ?

She glanced at her parents. They were having a long discussion with the customer service specialist.

Abby sighed.

She was just going to have to get used to the basics. There was really nothing more that she could do.

A half an hour later, the Hayes family walked out of the cell phone store.

"How did that happen?" Paul Hayes said in a stunned voice. He was carrying a very large shopping bag.

"I don't know," his wife replied. She also had a very large shopping bag and a dazed look on her face.

"Did someone secretly knock us out?" Paul Hayes asked. "Do we have doubles? Is this a case of alien possession?"

"I don't know," Olivia Hayes said again.

The four Hayes siblings looked at each other. Their parents weren't acting normal.

It took a lot to confuse their mother. She was a top-notch lawyer.

It took a lot to confuse their father, too. He was normally sensible, smart, and down-to-earth.

"So? What happened?" Isabel said. "You got cell phones, right?"

"Yes, but . . ." her father began.

"But what?" Eva prompted.

"But . . . oh, later!" her mother said. She rubbed her forehead.

"You *did* get the basic phone with the basic plan?" Eva said.

Her father unlocked the trunk and put down his bag. "You heard your mother," he said. "We'll go over everything when we get home."

"You didn't get anything *less* than basic, did you?" Abby asked her parents. She hoped that wasn't possible.

Her father slid into the front seat of the car. "You won't be unhappy," he promised.

"We got a deal," her mother said, almost apologetically.

Abby stared at her parents. She hardly dared to hope.

"When we get home," her father promised. "We'll tell you everything as soon as we get home."

Abby glanced at her sisters. "Do you think . . . ?" she whispered.

"I don't know," Eva whispered back. But her eyes had a hopeful gleam.

Alex leaned over the seat and tried to peer into the bags. But they were just out of reach.

"Don't touch those bags!" their father ordered.

"There's something fishy about this," Isabel muttered.

"I think it's good," Eva said under her breath.

Chapter 10

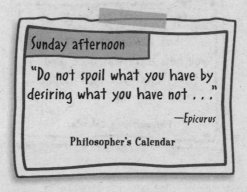

Sunday afternoon

"Do not spoil what you have by desiring what you have not . . ."

—Epicurus

Philosopher's Calendar

I don't want to spoil what I have, because it's more than I ever expected.

My parents didn't exactly get basic phones with a basic plan.

They got something better.

In my parents' eyes, it was a LOT better.

In my siblings' eyes, it was MUCH better.

In my eyes, it was just better.

*   *   *

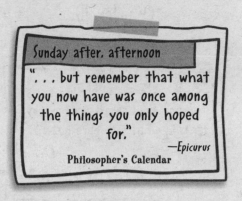

Sunday after. afternoon

". . . but remember that what you now have was once among the things you only hoped for."

—Epicurus

Philosopher's Calendar

My new cell phone is pretty basic. I don't want to mention it in the same breath as a Me-phone.

It's only distantly related to the sleek camera phones that my sisters, brother, and I were looking at in the store.

It's a poor cousin of Mason, Hannah, and Sophia's cell phones.

But it IS a cell phone.

Didn't I say a few days ago that I'd be happy with <u>any</u> cell phone at all?

Now I have it.

So I don't want to spoil what I have.

I don't want to BE spoiled, either! I don't want to be one of those kids who's always whining for something more. . . .

I don't want to be like Brianna, always demanding The Best. (Translation: "Most Expensive.")

I got what I said I wanted: a cell phone.

So what if it's basic?

Basic phones today aren't actually basic.

They have alarm clocks, calculators, calendars, stopwatches, notepads, voice recording, pop-up reminders, and text messaging, too.

That's a lot of good stuff.

My siblings and I especially like the text messaging.

And, best of all, our parents got us a Much-Better-Than-Basic plan.

We each have LOTS of minutes.

We have unlimited texting for the entire family.

HOORAY!

I can talk and text all I want. Isn't that the whole point?

But I have to tell the truth:

My new cell phone is kind of ugly.

Actually, it's really ugly.

I don't think I'll be flashing it in the school hallway tomorrow.

I won't be showing it off to all my friends.

I still wish I had a Me-phone. Or a camera phone. But I'm glad to have Any-phone.

P.S. If you think I'm mixed up . . . maybe I am!

Hayes Family Glad-O-Meter:

Eva: Very, very glad to have a cell

Isabel: So glad that she's at a loss for words for the first time in recorded history

Alex: Yelling with joy

Me: Mostly glad

Mom and Dad: Not glad. Feeling bad.

"We didn't mean to do it," my father stammered over and over again. "I don't know what came over us."

He made it sound like he had committed

a crime. Is it so terrible to buy cell phones with a decent plan for your family?

"How did we end up with such expensive monthly plans?" my mother said. "And we signed a two-year contract."

She sounded embarrassed, too. Like there was something wrong, instead of right.

"Five thousand monthly minutes!" my father said. "But at least the phones weren't too expensive."

"That customer service specialist could have sold ice in Iceland."

"Did we really want to do this?"

My siblings and I glanced at each other.

Our parents' conversation had taken an alarming turn.

Maybe they regretted their decision, but WE didn't.

"Never mind that," Eva interrupted. "We are all so happy with our new cell phones. Right, Abby?"

"Um, yeah," I said. "Pretty much."

"Thank you, Mom and Dad!" Alex said. He couldn't stop pressing buttons.

Probably he would wire his cell phone to run the washing machine or to light up the entire house.

"It's awesome, Mom and Dad!" Isabel said, looking up from hers. She was already texting one of her friends. "You're the best!"

"At least someone is glad about this," my father said in a gloomy voice.

"ALL of us love our cell phones," Eva said.

I didn't contradict her.

I sort of loved mine. And I sort of hated it.

I still wished it was a Me-phone, or something close. But it was definitely better than nothing at all!

Chapter 11

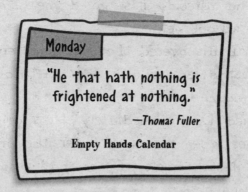

Wrong!

She that hath a cell phone is frightened at nothing.

Not even when she leaveth an important term paper on her desk at home.

She calleth her father on her cell phone and arrangeth for him to drop it off before class.

Problem solvedth.

Gloating Section:
Ha! So there! SEE?

75

I've had the cell phone for only a few hours and already it's saved me. I'm not even in school yet.

Yeah, I discovered I had forgotten the paper just after the bus took off down the highway.

I called Dad immediately. He's going to bring the paper to school later this morning.

(And if he forgets, I can call and remind him!)

Thank you, little cell phone. Even if you're cheap, hideous, and don't have a camera, you helped me out a lot this morning.

I can't wait to program my friends' numbers into your address book!

"I've got a new cell phone!" Abby announced to everyone she encountered.

She skipped down the hall, waving the phone in the air.

It was wrapped in a purple bandanna. Only the edge of the phone peeked out.

That way, she could show it off without showing it.

"New cell phone!" she cried, over and over, as she made her way toward her next class.

Halfway down the hall, Hannah joined her. "I can't believe your parents gave in!" she cried.

"Me, neither," Abby said. "Everyone in my family is in shock."

"This is great! Now we can talk to each other whenever we want!" Hannah pulled out her phone. "Let's program each other's numbers."

Abby unwrapped her phone. She would only show it to Hannah.

"It's the bottom-of-the-line model," she said apologetically. "That's all my parents would get us. Even though I offered to pay for a better phone."

Hannah smiled at the phone. "It's kind of cute."

"Like an armored car is cute," Abby retorted.

"Does it have a camera? Can you make movies with it?"

Abby shook her head.

"Too bad," Hannah said. "But it doesn't matter. You can use mine if you want."

"Thanks," Abby said. She glanced up. A few of their friends were approaching. Abby hurriedly shoved the phone into her pants pocket.

"I hear you have a new phone," Mason said. "Let me see it."

"Later," Abby said. "I have to go to class."

"Wait just a minute!" Mason pointed his cell at Abby and snapped her picture. "There!" he said with satisfaction. "I gotcha!"

He clicked a few more buttons. "You are now immortalized on the tiny screen," he announced.

"I am?" Abby peered at the photo.

Her curly red hair bounced wildly around her face, and she was smirking as she held her hands over the pocket where she had hidden her cell phone.

"I look goofy," she said.

"I think you look nice," Mason said. He grinned at her. "I don't know why you won't show me your cell."

Abby mumbled a few words of apology.

"Never mind," Mason said. "I know why."

"You do?" Did he have X-ray vision? Could he see the clunky phone hiding in her pocket?

She'd have to take it out sooner or later, though.

"You don't want to be like Brianna," Mason said. "No one can escape her bragging about HER phone."

"No," Abby agreed. She didn't want to brag like Brianna. But there *was* one way she wouldn't mind being like her!

* * *

At the end of the day, Hannah and Abby met in front of their lockers.

"Today I programmed thirty-two new numbers into my cell," Abby announced. "I texted half a dozen times, and my father delivered a paper I left at home."

No one had said anything rude about her phone, either. She had taken it out every time she programmed someone's number.

Abby slammed her locker door shut and picked up her backpack. "It was a very good day," she concluded.

"Want to come over to my house?" Hannah asked.

"I'd love to," Abby said. She opened her phone and touched two numbers to speed-dial her father's phone.

"Yes?" Her father sounded out of breath.

"Where are you, Dad?"

"Jogging on the Misty Acres trail."

"Can I go over to Hannah's?"

"Fine," her father said. "I'll pick you up at five thirty."

Abby shut the cell phone and smiled triumphantly. "Yes, I can!" she said.

"*Yes!*" Hannah cried.

Abby planted a kiss on the screen of her cell phone.

A day or two ago, she wouldn't have been able to get hold of her father so easily or quickly.

If he had been out jogging, she wouldn't have been able to reach him at all.

She would have had to take the bus straight home and forget about Hannah.

Abby slid her cell phone into the pocket of her cargo pants. Then she and Hannah strolled out of the school together.

"This is just like old times," Abby said, as they walked down the street.

"It makes me realize how much I miss seeing you," Hannah agreed. "I wish you hadn't moved out of our neighborhood."

"I wish that every day," Abby said.

A phone began to ring.

"Is that yours . . . ?" Hannah asked.

"I think it's yours," Abby said.

Hannah flipped open her phone. "Hello? I'm walking home with Abby. Yeah." She was silent for a moment. "Okay."

"Sorry about that," Hannah said to Abby as she put the phone back in her pocket. "My mother wants me to put the clothes in the dryer when we get home."

"Chores," Abby said.

"Yeah," Hannah said. She let out a long breath. "So what were we talking about?"

"Um, I forget," Abby said. "Old times?"

"Oh, right, old times," Hannah said. "I was just saying that . . ."

Another cell phone ring interrupted her.

This time, it was Abby's.

Sophia was on the other line. She wanted today's English homework.

"I'll have to give it to you later," Abby said. "I'm walking home with Hannah now."

"Gosh, I'm sorry . . ." Abby said to Hannah, but now Hannah's phone was ringing again.

"Good grief," Hannah said. She glanced at the display. "I have to take it," she said. "It's my father."

She listened for a few moments. Then she said, "Yes, Dad, I'll get everything ready. Okay. Good-bye."

"More chores?" Abby asked.

"More chores," Hannah groaned. "I have to chop vegetables. Don't let your parents use your cell phone as a chore reminder tool."

"Thanks for the tip," Abby said. "I won't."

"They'll figure it out sooner or later, though," Hannah said in a gloomy tone.

The two girls walked for a few minutes in silence.

"So what *were* we talking about?" Hannah asked Abby after a moment. "Now I've really forgotten!"

"That this is just like old times?" Abby said. Her cell phone began to ring.

"Do you *have* to get it?" Hannah said.

"Um, yeah, I think I do," Abby said. "It's my sister Eva."

She opened the phone and pressed the SEND button. "Hello?"

"*Hello?*" Hannah said, as her phone began to ring again.

As they each held their cell phones to their ears, the two friends looked at each other.

Well, no, it wasn't just like old times.

It wasn't like old times at all.

When you were away from your friends, cell phones were a blessing.

But when you were *with* your friends, they were a constant annoyance.

Abby wasn't sure she liked this at all.

Chapter 12

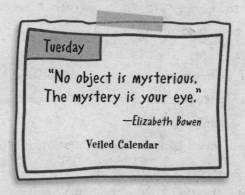

Tuesday

"No object is mysterious.
The mystery is your eye."

—Elizabeth Bowen

Veiled Calendar

My eye isn't a mystery. It's just an eye in my head, next to its twin eye.

Are my twin eyes like the twins, Eva and Isabel?

They look very much alike, they're part of the same family, and they don't want to exist without each other.

But my eyes aren't really like my twin sisters.

They don't argue and fight like Isabel and Eva do.

They don't stomp into their rooms and slam their doors.

They don't refuse to speak to each other.

And it's a good thing, too! If my eyes refused to cooperate, I wouldn't be able to see my cell phone!

The true mystery is my cell phone.
A few inches of modern technology have completely changed my life.
My cell phone has changed my emotions.
It has changed my habits.
It has changed my thoughts, too.
Not only that, but cell phones are now changing my family.
Is this good or is this bad? Or is it both?

Cell Phone Central:
Last night was our first "cell phone dinner."
It was like me and Hannah, only times six.
When the Hayes family sat down at the table, everyone's phones started ringing at once.

Question: What do six cell phones with six different ringtones and six highly important conversations add up to?
Answer: Pandemonium.

*   *   *

<u>Definition</u>: Pandemonium: a "wild and noisy disorder or confusion; an uproar."

A "wild and noisy disorder" describes last night's Hayes family dinner to a T.

To tell the truth, our family dinners are usually wild, noisy, disorderly, and uproarious.

Especially when Eva and Isabel argue.

There was a big change last night, however.

Usually our pandemonium comes from talking, arguing, and laughing with <u>each other</u>.

But at our first sit-down cell phone dinner, we talked, laughed, and argued with a <u>bunch of invisible people</u>.

Eva and Isabel set up rehearsal times and practice sessions, and gossiped with their friends.

Alex discussed cell phones on his cell phone with other technology fanatics.

Mom took a stream of business-related phone calls.

Dad chatted with his relatives all over the country.

I fielded questions about today's homework.

It just didn't feel like the Hayes family anymore.

We usually share our day over dinner.

We show the other people in our family that we care about them.

We look into each others' eyes and communicate.

Sure, we're grumpy sometimes, but we look at, speak, and respond to each other.

We don't pretend that no one else exists.

We don't ignore each other.

We don't act like a few square inches of shiny technology is more important than our family members.

But . . . shouldn't we feel closer to each other now that we share a love cell phones?

Shouldn't I feel happier that my family has also become cell-phone crazy?

Strangely enough, I don't.

I feel much more unhappy.

*   *   *

It was bad enough that we had to move to Misty Acres, but now my family was changing, too!

I didn't like it!

So I did the only thing I could think of.

I stood up, dinged my fork on my glass, and made an announcement.

"Hear ye, hear ye!" I said. "I propose a new Hayes family rule. No more cell phones at the dinner table."

No one was listening. They all had their ears glued to their cells.

My father carried a pie to the table (while talking to his third cousin, twice removed).

"Turn them off, everyone!" I commanded in a loud voice. "Silence your cell phones!"

I thought it was a brave announcement.

My family looked at me like they thought I was crazy.

But I got their attention.

Several cell phones were slowly lowered. A few ringers were even silenced.

"This is really you, Abby?" my sister Isabel said. "My little sister, Abby I-Want-A-Me-Phone Hayes?"

"You started this, Abby," Eva said, as she hung up on her call. "Don't change your mind now."

"I'm not changing my mind," I protested. "But why does everyone have to talk straight through dinner?"

"You've had three phone calls in the last fifteen minutes," Isabel said to me. "You're just as bad as everyone else."

"So?" I said. "That's not the point."

"What is the point?" Alex asked.

"I think we should turn off our cell phones at dinner so we can talk to each other," I said, turning to a parent for support. "Right, Mom?"

My mother didn't leap to my defense.

"I get very important calls," she said, a bit defensively. "I have to take them."

As if to prove the point, her cell phone rang.

"Abby, you persuaded us to get the phones and now you're telling us to silence them," Isabel said with her usual cold logic. "Do you really think that's fair? Do you think it's reasonable? Do you think it's just?"

"Yes!" I said.

My father looked worried. "I think Abby might be right," he said, getting off his call.

"Thank you, Dad," I breathed.

"But I don't agree!" Eva cried. "With Abby, I mean. No way, no how."

"Me, neither," Alex said. "Cell phones rule."

"That's the problem," I said.

"If you ask me . . ." Isabel began.

"Haven't you said enough already?" I began. "You always hog the conversation, Isabel."

"Shut up, Abby," Eva interrupted.

"Now wait a minute. . . ." my father said.

"Kids, kids," my mother said. "Must you raise your voices?"

"Yes!" I shouted.

The Hayes family erupted in angry arguments.

HOORAY!

A good old-fashioned fight!

We hadn't forgotten how to be Hayeses.

We were speaking to each other again!

(Well, actually yelling, but who cares.)

Question: Will someone have to pick a fight every night to get us off our cell phones?

Answer: Not clear yet.

But I hope Mom and Dad will enact a new family rule. Like making family dinner time a Cell-free Zone.

Please, Mom and Dad?

Please don't let cell phones ruin our lives.

Chapter 13

Wednesday

"We must not say every mistake is a foolish one."

—Cicero

It's a Blunder-ful World Calendar

Oh, yeah?

<u>Number One Foolish Mistake</u>:

Letting Brianna catch a glimpse of my new cell phone on the school bus this morning.

Of course, I didn't intend for her to see it.

But it rang and I had to answer it.

It was my father, reminding me about a thank-you note to my grandmother that I had promised to write today.

When I hung up the phone, Brianna was staring at me. "What is _that_?"

"Uh, my new cell phone," I said.

"You call that a cell phone?"

"I know it's not a Me-phone," I began, "but it . . ."

"Don't even think of comparing it to my Me-phone!" Brianna interrupted. "Don't mention them in the same breath."

"Aren't you even a little bit happy for me?" I asked. "I mean, I didn't think I'd get any cell phone at all. . . ." My voice trailed off.

Brianna wasn't listening. She was watching a podcast, of, who else?

Herself!

"Hush, Abby," she said, putting a manicured finger to her glossy lips. "My big number is coming up next."

Number Two Foolish Mistake:
Expecting Brianna to be happy for me. Or at least expecting her to _pretend_ she was happy for me.

<u>Number Three Foolish Mistake</u>:
Forgetting <u>everything</u> when I see the Me-phone.

I forget how annoying cell phones can be.
I forget how, just last night, I asked everyone to turn their phones off during dinner.
I forget how I sometimes think that cell phones are overrated.
I forget that Brianna can't think about anything but hers, truly.

And each time I see it, I fall in love with the Me-phone.
It is beyond awesome.
It is one of the seven technological wonders of the world.
It is a sleek, shining, glittering, gorgeous device that no one can resist, especially me.

<u>Number Four Foolish Mistake</u>:
Wishing that Brianna would let me hold her Me-phone again!

She forgot all about me.

She watched the podcast of herself over and over and over, until we reached the school.

Abby turned on the water in the school bathroom sink and squirted her hands with liquid soap.

As she held them under the running water, she grimaced at her reflection in the mirror.

Maybe one day she'd look in the mirror and see a whole new person: someone who loved math, who had a great singing voice, who was the oldest child in her family, and who owned a Me-phone.

But there was the same Abby, a middle child, who wasn't good at math, couldn't sing, and had a cell phone that didn't even take pictures.

Abby dried off her hands and checked the time on her phone.

It was ten twenty-two. The bell was about to ring. Abby was going to be late for her next class.

But it didn't matter. It was only study hall. She wouldn't get in trouble if she arrived a few minutes late.

She ran her hands through her hair and turned to leave. But then she noticed that someone had scrawled some graffiti on one of the walls.

"Brianna is a star!" it said. The words were written in lipstick.

She probably wrote that herself, Abby thought. *Or got someone else to do it for her.*

She put down her backpack and tried to wipe it off with a paper towel. But she only succeeded in smearing it on the wall.

Now it really looked awful. But the girls' room always did, anyway.

Abby threw the towel in the wastebasket. She'd tell the custodian if she saw him.

As she prepared to leave, she saw something gleaming on the floor. It was partially covered by a crumpled towel. Abby nudged it with her foot.

Probably nothing, she thought. A chewing gum wrapper. A piece of junk jewelry. Someone's shiny old book cover.

When she saw what it really was, she drew in a long, startled breath.

Then she knelt down to get a closer look.

A brand-new, shiny Me-phone lay on the bathroom floor.

Abby picked it up and cradled it in her hands. She gazed at it in wonder.

"How did you get here?" she murmured. "Did you fall out of a backpack? Did you slip from a pocket? Were you knocked off the sink?

"And how could *anyone* forget you or not notice that you were gone?"

She already knew who the phone belonged to.

There was only one person in middle school who owned a Me-phone.

And besides, it was hard to miss Brianna's face smiling professionally from the screen.

Abby could almost hear her saying, "I'm the best."

She tried to navigate away from Brianna's photo, but the screen kept shuffling glossy portraits of her on horseback, in a limousine, in a ruffled ball gown.

Suddenly, the phone rang. An unfamiliar name flashed on the screen.

What do I do now? Abby thought in a panic. *Should I answer it? Let it ring? Do I leave the phone here? Take it with me?*

Perhaps Brianna was about to come flying through the door, searching for her beloved Me-phone.

Abby could hand it to her and say, "I found it lying on the floor near the trash, Brianna."

That would be very satisfying.

Of course, she could always leave the phone where she found it. But what if someone stole it?

She really ought to take the phone and return it to Brianna. That was the best thing to do.

Abby silenced the ringer and slipped the Me-phone into a zippered backpack pocket.

Then she went out the door and headed for study hall.

Abby tried to study for her social studies quiz.

She read a paragraph or two from her book, but the words wouldn't register in her mind.

She couldn't help wondering if Brianna had noticed yet that her Me-phone was missing.

Wouldn't she have sounded a fire alarm or made a schoolwide announcement?

If Brianna knew that she had lost her cell, she'd make sure that everyone in the school was looking for it.

But if she didn't know, if she hadn't noticed, why couldn't Abby keep the Me-phone a little while longer?

Abby turned a page. She stared at pictures of past presidents and buildings that no longer existed.

Those presidents didn't have Me-phones. They didn't even have cell phones or landlines.

If Abby had a Me-phone, she'd *never* forget or lose it anywhere. Especially not on the bathroom floor.

If I keep the Me-phone for one or two hours, would Brianna really know the difference? she asked herself. *Especially if she hasn't even noticed it's gone.*

Abby could lock herself in the bathroom or find a deserted spot in the library so she could check out the Me-phone more thoroughly.

She didn't want to hurt it.

She definitely didn't want to steal it.

She just wanted to imagine that it was hers for a few moments before she returned it.

And then she would find Brianna and return it. No one would know; no one would be hurt.

"What would you do," Abby asked Hannah and Sophia at lunch, "if you found something that belonged to someone else?"

"Return it," Hannah said promptly.

"That's right," Sophia agreed.

Abby twirled a length of curly red hair around her fingers.

The Me-phone had been burning a hole in her backpack since she found it. It had been several hours already, but she still hadn't given it back to Brianna.

For one thing, she kept hoping for a few more minutes with the Me-phone.

For another, she wasn't sure that Brianna had missed it yet.

Abby glanced across the room. As usual, Brianna was holding court in the midst of a group of admirers.

"I've starred in five commercials this year," Brianna bragged loud enough for the entire cafeteria to hear. "I'm the top model for the Me-First Modeling Agency."

Her group of admirers clapped loudly.

"If you want an autographed color photograph, I have one or two in my backpack," Brianna offered. "They're already collectors' items."

Hannah stared at Brianna. "She's too much," she said.

"Over the top," Sophia agreed.

"Seriously annoying," Abby agreed. She took a bite of her sandwich.

"I have another question for you," she said after a moment. "Is it okay to hold on to something for a few hours before you return it?"

"You mean, on purpose?" Sophia said. "I don't think so."

"Even if she, I mean, *the person,* seems perfectly happy without it?" Abby said. "In fact, I'm not sure they deserve it."

"That's not the point," Hannah said. "If it's not yours, you should give it back right away."

Abby flushed.

"Is this one of those 'good choice/bad choice' questions for English class?" Sophia asked. "Are you writing an essay?"

"Um, yeah, sure," Abby said. She pushed her sandwich away, unfinished.

"Good luck," Hannah said.

"Yeah, thanks," Abby mumbled.

She knew that she had already kept the Me-phone too long. But she just couldn't give it back yet.

There wasn't enough privacy in school. She needed to take it out behind the locked door of her room at home.

At the very latest, she promised herself, *I'll return it to Brianna first thing tomorrow morning.*

Chapter 14

Wednesday evening

"There is no greater
disaster than greed."

—Lao-tzu

Full Moon Calendar

Um, yes.
I wish I hadn't been so greedy.
I wish I hadn't kept the Me-phone.
Because now it's getting harder to give up.

When I rode the school bus
home today, Brianna sat down
next to me.
The Me-phone was in
my backpack. It seemed to
cry out, "Brianna, I'm here!
I'm here!"

Brianna!

But I ignored its cry. It would have been too awkward to give it back on the school bus.

I mean, how would I explain why I hadn't returned it earlier? And what would the kids around us say?

And, honestly, I _really_ wanted to take the Me-phone home. In spite of my better judgment.

So when Brianna sat down next to me, I already felt guilty.

I wanted to get up and run, but you can't escape on a school bus.

Especially when you're in the window seat and someone sits down next to you in the aisle seat.

I felt even worse when I saw Brianna's face. Her eyes were red and her makeup was smeared.

"Abby, it's a tragedy!" she cried, dabbing at her nose with a tissue. "The worst thing has happened!"

"What?" I asked, although I was pretty sure that I knew the answer.

"My Me-phone is missing," she sobbed. "I had to make a call a few minutes ago. . . . I went to get it out of my backpack. It wasn't there!"

(Hey? What took her so long? I would have noticed in, like, six seconds.)

"I'm, uh, really sorry," I stammered.

"I'm not even supposed to be on the school bus," she went on. "I was supposed to call my mother. . . ."

From inside my backpack, the Me-phone shouted at me, "Give me back! Right now!"

But I closed my ears to it, even as a mascara-stained tear slid down Brianna's cheek.

"What am I going to do, Abby?" she wailed.

"Do you want to borrow my cell?" I mumbled.

"Thanks, you're sweet." Brianna dabbed at her eyes. "But my mother has a brand-new number. She programmed it into my Me-phone this morning!"

I felt horrible. Really, really horrible.

But I still didn't give the phone back.

      *   *   *

Now I'm home and I can't even look at the Me-phone.

I don't want to take it out of my backpack.

I don't want to scroll through its options.

I don't want to look at it; I don't want to see it; I don't want to remember that I have it.

The truth is, I can't face it.

All I can think about is how unhappy Brianna looked when she got off the bus. It's all my fault that she missed her ride.

How did I ever mess things up so badly?

I feel so guilty that I don't even want to use MY cell phone!

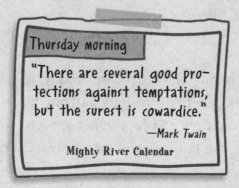

Thursday morning

"There are several good protections against temptations, but the surest is cowardice."

—Mark Twain

Mighty River Calendar

Ha! I wish that I had been more cowardly.

I wish that I had been SO cowardly that I left Brianna's Me-phone where I found it on the bathroom floor.

Then I wouldn't have all these problems.

But now, the really strange thing is, I'm worried that I'm TOO cowardly to return it.

In a few minutes, I'm leaving for school.

I MUST be courageous. I MUST give the Me-phone back to Brianna as <u>soon</u> as I see her.

As she stepped off the school bus Thursday morning, Abby felt dizzy and sick to her stomach.

The symptoms had begun when the bus pulled into the parking lot.

They got worse when she caught sight of the middle school.

Brianna hadn't ridden the bus today.

That was good. Abby had half an hour reprieve. She had more time to prepare her speech.

But now she had arrived at school. There was no turning back.

Abby not only had to return the Me-phone; she had to tell Brianna the truth. Well, *mostly* the truth.

Abby planned to omit only one small fact: the day and time she had found the Me-phone.

"I found your Me-phone in the first-floor girls' bathroom," Abby said silently over and over. "It was lying on the floor under a paper towel."

Would Brianna believe the truth? Or would she say, "That's impossible! You're making it up!"

The more Abby thought about it, the sicker she felt.

Maybe Brianna would be so happy to see her Me-phone again that she wouldn't care.

Maybe she wouldn't argue with Abby.

Maybe she would just say, "Thank you."

As Abby entered the school, her stomach clenched in dread. If Brianna guessed that she had kept the phone overnight . . .

"I didn't mean any harm, Brianna," Abby might say. Or, "Please don't be too upset. Your Me-phone is safely back in your hands."

Abby barely responded to the greetings of her friends. Instead, she scanned the halls for Brianna.

She found her in front of the main office, tacking a notice to the bulletin board.

I have to do it, Abby said to herself. *I can't put it off another minute.*

"Everyone knows that it's not easy to fool me," were Brianna's first words to Abby. "Don't you agree?"

"Um, of course," Abby said. This wasn't the conversation starter she had hoped for.

Abby took a deep breath. "I have something to tell you, Brianna. . . ."

Brianna cut her off. "Never mind that. Your little news will have to wait. I have found out the truth."

"You have?" Abby's voice cracked. Had Brianna seen through her already? "Brianna, I didn't mean . . . it was all a mistake. . . ."

"No mistake about it," Brianna said. "My Mephone was stolen."

Abby went pale.

"Naturally, you're shocked and outraged," Brianna said. "As are all right-thinking people. But justice will be done!"

Brianna brandished her fist. "You must help me, Abby."

"*Me?* Help you?" Abby stammered. She felt dizzy with relief. "Yes, Brianna. Of course."

Brianna pointed to the bulletin board.

In large sparkly pink letters, she had offered a cash reward for the return of the Me-phone.

"If you identify the guilty culprit, you will also have my eternal gratitude and a free autographed picture," the poster promised.

"Isn't this, um, a bit extreme?" Abby said.

"The entire school is up in arms," Brianna said. "This crime has chilled our collective blood."

"Are you *sure* your Me-phone was stolen?" Abby pleaded. "I mean, maybe you dropped it somewhere. Like in a classroom or a bathroom . . ."

"Never!" Brianna cried. "I'd never, *ever* let my Me-phone out of my sight for a moment. How can you even think that?"

"I, uh, well . . ." Abby took another deep breath and tried to summon up some courage.

Or some cowardice.

Or whatever would make her return the Me-phone right this minute. This had gone on long enough.

"*I* know the real truth, Brianna," Abby began. "Your phone wasn't stolen at all. . . ."

"Oh, Abby." Brianna dismissed her with a wave of her hand. "Stop trying to make me feel better."

"I'm *not,* really," Abby protested. "Listen to what I have to say."

"The sixth cousin of my mother's uncle's sister-in-law's nephew's fiancée is a private eye," Brianna interrupted. "His keen detective mind is on the case right now. He'll find the perpetrator."

Abby felt alarmed all over again. "But what if whoever has your phone didn't mean to take it?"

"Don't be silly! Of course they meant to take it," Brianna said. "*Everyone* wants my Me-phone. Even you, Abby."

Abby turned pale again. Then she slowly backed away. "See you later," she muttered. "I have to go to my class."

"Don't take it personally!" Brianna called after her. "I know that you'd never do anything like that."

Chapter 15

Friday

"The more wealth, the more worry."

—Hillel

Bling Calendar

Ever since I found Brianna's Me-phone, all I do is worry.

Yesterday at noon, Brianna leafleted the cafeteria.

Just in case anyone had missed the bright pink posters on every single bulletin board in the school, we all received a flyer featuring a glossy color picture of Brianna and her Me-phone.

The flyer offered a cash reward for the return of Brianna's Me-phone.

It also deputized every student in the school to make a "citizen's arrest."

If that wasn't enough, Brianna also made a public announcement about a "schoolwide crime wave."

"Watch your cell phones, everyone!" she warned. "Put away your PDAs. Hide your personal electronics."

All over the school, you could hear the sound of kids zipping their cell phones and portable handheld gaming devices into their backpacks.

Brianna also initiated a schoolwide search.

"We will look in backpacks," she cried. "We will look in lockers. We will look in desks."

"There is a ruthless criminal on the loose," she said. "No one is safe until he or she is caught."

"This is Brianna," she concluded. "Serving my public. Please nominate me for the School Citizenship Award this month. Over and out."

Help! Help! Help!

All I meant to do was spend a couple

extra hours with the Me-phone. And now I'm a "perpetrator," a "ruthless criminal," and a "culprit."

Eight hundred and seventy-two students in the middle school want to win the cash reward that Brianna is offering.

Any of my friends who discover the Me-phone in my backpack can arrest me.

A professional detective is on the case.

I feel like a rat in a maze.

If I'm ever found with the Me-phone, it's all over for me!

Must not panic. Must stay calm. Must think.

Think! Think!

If I can get the Me-phone back to Brianna, she will call off the detective. My friends will no longer try to win the cash reward.

Everything will go back to normal . . . if ONLY I can return the Me-phone.

I need a plan.

*   *   *

Plan A

Hide Me-phone in paper bag.

Leave bag where Brianna will find it.

Watch Brianna reunite joyfully with her Me-phone.

Plan A in Action

First thing Friday morning, I place the paper bag on the bench at the bus stop.

Brianna sits down right next to it.

Hooray!

"Look, a paper bag," I say. "What do you think is in it?"

"Something disgusting, I'm sure," Brianna replies.

"Maybe it's a million dollars," I suggest.

"Trust me, it isn't." Brianna laughs. Then she gets up and climbs into the school bus, which has just arrived.

I quickly put the paper bag and Me-phone in my backpack.

Plan A is absurd and awkward.

114

Plan B

Try to arrive in bathroom before Brianna does.

Leave Me-phone on sink for her to find.

Slip out before Brianna reunites joyfully with her Me-phone.

Plan B in Action

Seven bathroom passes in two and a half hours.

And still no Brianna!

Teachers begin to give me suspicious looks.

The sink is wet and not a good place to leave expensive gadgets.

I lurk in bathroom, washing hands until they are raw.

Plan B is bad.

Plan C

Wrap Me-phone in paper napkin.

Secretly place it on Brianna's lunch tray.

Along with several hundred other middle schoolers eating mystery meat or putrid pizza, watch Brianna joyfully reunite with Me-phone.

Plan C in Action
Napkin not big enough to cover Me-phone.

Tape two napkins together over cell phone. Looks very suspicious, not to mention stupid.

Walk over to Brianna's lunch tray.

Brianna sitting in front of lunch tray, eating lettuce.

Think of handing Me-phone to her, anyway.

Think better of it.

Hold napkin-covered Me-phone behind back and slowly walk away.

Plan C is crazy, cuckoo, and almost catastrophic.

Plan D
Enter classroom early.

Put Me-phone on Brianna's desk.

Watch Brianna . . . well, you know!

Plan D in Action

Enter classroom early.

Find Brianna's desk.

Take out napkin-wrapped Me-phone.

Just in time, realize that room isn't empty.

Laugh loudly. Whisk Me-phone back in zippered pocket.

Plan D is downright deranged. And so am I.

Plan E?

Oh, forget it.

There's no way I'm doing Plan E.

Plan E is excessive, extreme, and exhausting.

I hereby eliminate it.

Chapter 16

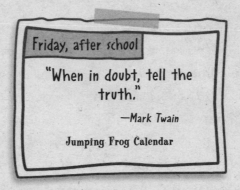

Friday, after school

"When in doubt, tell the truth."

—Mark Twain

Jumping Frog Calendar

Yeah. Just tell the truth, the whole truth,
and nothing but the truth.
Why didn't I do that in the first place?
What was stopping me?

Abby climbed the wide polished steps leading up to
Brianna's door, and rang the gold-plated doorbell.

The front door swung open. "Abby?" Brianna didn't
look pleased to see her. She was wearing sweatpants
and a T-shirt. There was a mud mask on her face.

"I wasn't expecting visitors," she snapped. "You
really should have called first, you know."

Wordlessly, Abby reached into her backpack. She took out the Me-phone and handed it to Brianna.

Brianna's mouth dropped open. A series of tiny cracks appeared in the mud mask.

"*What?*" she gasped. "You found my Me-phone? Oh, Abby, you've found it!"

Brianna ran her fingers over the phone. She kissed it once and brushed off a tiny fleck of mud that had dropped on the screen. Then she turned it on, touched all the buttons, and checked the call log.

"No one's used it," she said with satisfaction. "It's even charged."

"Well, now you have it," Abby said, letting out a long breath. She had done it. It hadn't been that terrible, either.

Was it really going to be that easy?

Abby took a few steps backward. "I'm so happy for you."

It was probably one of the most sincere statements that she had ever made to Brianna.

"Wait! You can't just leave like that!" Brianna cried.

"But, um, I have chores . . . and, um, lots of home-work. And your face mask . . ."

"I'll redo it," Brianna said crisply. "But you haven't told me anything. Where did you find my Me-phone? Who took it?"

Abby took a deep breath. "I found it at school," she said. "In the girls' bathroom."

Brianna snorted. "No way!"

"It was on the floor under the sink," Abby continued. "Covered by a crumpled-up paper towel."

"The thief must have hidden it there," Brianna said. "Very clever. No one would think of looking there."

"Maybe," Abby said hesitantly.

"Did you see any suspicious people lurking about?"

Abby shook her head.

"Did you dust the Me-phone for fingerprints?"

"Of course not!"

Brianna sighed. "That's a shame."

Abby twisted a lock of hair around her finger. "But this is a happy ending, Brianna," she said, starting to breathe again.

"How can I ever thank you?" Brianna said. "If you ever want an autographed picture of me, just ask. I'll even give you a free poster."

"Oh, that's all right," Abby said.

Brianna clapped her hand to her forehead. The mask cracked more deeply. "I forgot!" she cried. "The cash reward! You so totally deserve it."

"No, no!" Abby said hastily. "I don't want any reward."

The Me-phone began to ring.

Brianna eagerly pressed the SEND button. "Hello? Brianna Central," she said. "*The* Brianna speaking."

The speakerphone was on.

"Brianna, I saw your Me-phone in school." A girl's voice boomed loudly out of the Me-phone.

"Where?" Brianna demanded. "Abby Hayes just brought it to me."

"Well, she was the one who had it."

Abby slowly began to back down the stairs.

The girl snickered. "She was talking to it in the library yesterday."

"Is this for real?" Brianna said to Abby.

Abby froze.

"I'm so sorry, Brianna," Abby said, although she knew that didn't begin to cover it.

On the other end of the Me-phone, the girl said, "I *told* you . . ."

"Oh, shut up," Brianna said, ending the call.

She stared at Abby for a very long moment. "My Me-phone's been missing for three days," she finally said.

Abby waited for the rush of angry words. She knew she deserved all of them.

But Brianna didn't seem upset. "You, Abby?" she said.

"Me," Abby said miserably.

"I didn't know you had it in you."

"Me, neither."

The worst thing was, Abby still wanted the Me-phone. But she'd never take it again, that was for sure.

"So, how did you like it?" Brianna asked.

"Like it?" Abby repeated. "Do you mean did I like taking the Me-phone? No, I didn't. But I love the Me-phone itself."

"You don't understand." Brianna smiled. "I mean how did you like pretending to be me?"

"What?"

"I know that's why you took the Me-phone," Brianna said.

"I didn't, really . . ."

"You wanted to know how it felt to be me, to be the best, to have the best of everything," Brianna went on.

"Good-bye, Brianna. I'm *really* sorry about your phone. I'll never do it again." Abby turned and began to walk quickly toward her home.

Brianna's laugh followed her.

Is it true? Abby asked herself. *Am I really turning into Brianna?*

She wasn't — she couldn't be — she didn't want to. *Never!*

Even if she had a hundred Me-phones, she'd never be Brianna.

Abby pulled her basic, ugly cell phone out of her pocket and stared at it, trying to reassure herself.

Such a plain, ordinary thing. She still wanted a Me-phone. But this one would have to do for a while.

Abby pressed the speed dial for Hannah's number.

"Hello, Hannah?" she said. "I have a lot to tell you. . . ."

DON'T MISS THE NEXT BOOK:

The Amazing Days of Abby Hayes #20:
Sealed with a Kiss

Start reading now for a sneak peek!

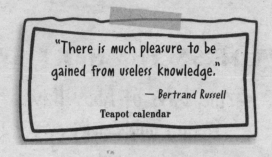

WRONG!!!

There is NO pleasure to be gained from useless knowledge.

Useless Knowledge: Eva is in love.

So where is the pleasure?

One: I haven't been able to tease Eva.

Two: I haven't gotten Eva to do my chores.

Three: I haven't dropped any tantalizing hints to Isabel.

There's been no pleasure gained at all.

In fact, it's the opposite.

Isabel thinks I'm holding out on her. Eva is mad at me.

This knowledge isn't useless!

It's worse than useless!

It's uncomfortable, awkward, and it gets me in trouble with my siblings.

It was the middle of the school day. Abby hurried from one class to another, trying to avoid looking at the Smooch cards.

They reminded her not only of Valentine's Day now, but also of her older sisters. And *that* reminded her that they were both very annoyed with her.

Somehow she had gotten put in the middle again. Was that because she was a middle child?

Abby sighed as another Smooch card reared up in front of her. This one was dangling from a seventh grade girl's backpack.

Smooch cards were everywhere.

Original Smooch card artwork was on display in the cafeteria; teachers had thumbtacked Smooch cards to their bulletin boards.

Students glued them on notebook covers, were hanging them in their lockers; one boy had even made a hat of Smooch cards.

Everyone in middle school seemed to be buying them, displaying them, or exchanging them.

"What's the matter, Abby?" her friend Sophia asked. "You look upset about something."

Sophia's long, dark hair was pulled into a ponytail. Her backpack was decorated with slogans and buttons.

Sophia wanted to be an artist. She spent every spare moment drawing in a blank notebook she carried everywhere.

"Oh, it's nothing," Abby said. "Just an overdose of Smooch cards, that's all."

"But they're so cute!" Sophia cried. "And so romantic, too!"

"And they help save the earth," Abby finished with a sigh. "I know all about it."

Brianna interrupted them.

"Hey, everyone," she began. "I have an important announcement!"

"Oh, really?" Abby said.

Brianna only made important announcements about one subject: herself.

"I have a new outfit for the Valentine's dance," she bragged. "A gold cashmere sweater, a matching flounced skirt — and even a new coat."

"Congratulations," Sophia said.

Brianna flashed her broadest movie star smile. Then she waltzed over to another group of girls to tell them the news.

"Brought to you by the Brianna channel," Abby said in a fake-newscaster voice. "All Brianna, all the time."

"If it doesn't exist, Brianna will soon start it," Sophia commented.

"What were we talking about?" Abby said. "Before Brianna interrupted us, I mean."

"I forgot."

"Smooch cards," Abby said. She made a face. She shouldn't have brought up the subject again. Oh, well. "Have you gotten any?"

"Not yet," Sophia said. "But I've sent a few."

"To *boys*?" Abby said in astonishment.

She couldn't believe it. Sophia was very shy. "Or *a* boy?"

Sophia suddenly looked embarrassed. "Well, uh, yeah. . ."

"Who?" Abby asked.

Sophia shook her head.

"I get it," Abby said. "You want to keep it secret. My sister. . ."

She stopped herself. She couldn't blurt out Eva's secret to anyone else.

"Are you going to the dance?" Abby said, to change the subject. "Hannah is getting a group of friends together."

Sophia's blush deepened.

"You're going with a *boy*?"

"I don't know," Sophia admitted. "I hope so."

"Wow," Abby said. "Wow." She didn't know what else to say.

"Are you going?" Sophia asked her.

"I don't think so," Abby choked out.

"Not even with Hannah?" Sophia said.

Abby shook her head.

"Are you going to hide out until February 15th?" Sophia asked. "Or wear a paper bag over your head?"

"Why can't things stay the same?" Abby burst out. "I liked Valentine's Day the way it *used* to be."

Sophia was quiet for a moment. "I like all the changes," she admitted. "I like this part of growing up."

The bell rang.

"Are you going to study hall?" Sophia asked.

"I'm going to my locker to get some books first," Abby said.

The two girls waved to each other and hurried off in opposite directions.

Abby fiddled with the catch on the lock. Why did it *always* stick when she was in a hurry?

She missed elementary school, where nobody had lockers.

After the third try, it released. Abby yanked the door open, grabbed the books she needed, and was about to slam the door shut again.

But then she saw the envelope.

She leaned over to pick it up. She didn't recognize the handwriting.

It looked like an invitation to a party — hopefully not a Valentine's Day party.

Abby turned it over. There was no return address or name on the envelope.

Then she tore it open. And stared in shock.

Someone had sent her a Smooch card.

WHAT GOES UP MUST COME DOWN

#18

The Hayes family is visiting Paris, the City of Lights. Too bad it's also the City of Fights! All the bickering is driving Abby up the wall. Things get really interesting, then scary, then wonderful when she and her sisters tour the city on their own.

THE BEST IS YET TO COME

Abby's peaceful vacation is disturbed thanks to so... unexpected houseguests. Can her perfect summer saved?

TWO SPECIAL EDITIONS
two color inserts!

KNOWLEDGE IS POWER

Abby's starting sixth grade at last! She thinks she's ready for anything—until she makes a mortifying mistake on her first day. Can Abby make it better? Or will one mistake follow her through the rest of middle school?

A Little Sister Can Be A Big Pain—Especially If She Has Magical Powers!

candy apple books

Drama Queen

I've Got a Secret

Confessions of a
Bitter Secret Santa

The Boy Next Door

The Sister Switch

The Accidental
Cheerleader

The Babysitting Wars

Star-Crossed

SCHOLASTIC

www.scholastic.com/candyapple

CAN

read them all!

Accidentally
Fabulous

Accidentally
Famous

Accidentally
Fooled

Accidentally
Friends

to Be a Girly Girl
Just Ten Days

Miss Popularity

Miss Popularity
Goes Camping

Making Waves

e, Starring Me!

Juicy Gossip

Callie for President

Totally Crushed

ARE YOU READY FOR MIDDLE SCHOOL?

After studying her Middle School handbook, Jenny is totally ready for sixth grade— she and her BFF, Addie, are sure to have a blast!

But when Jenny meets Addie at their lockers the next day, it looks like Addie has other plans— that don't include her. Is Addie ditching Jenny for the Pops—the coolest seventh graders in the school?